AF304505

Defoe Abbott Marx Hardy Melville Montaigne Machiavelli Haggard Chesterton Cooper Emerson Joyce Austen Hugo Eliot Grimm
Stoker Carroll Christie Maupassant Byron Engels Schiller Molière
Wilde Garnett Fitzgerald Einstein Hawthorne Smith Kafka Hall
Goethe Dostoyevsky Willis
Baum Cotton Henry Kipling Doyle
Leslie Dumas Flaubert Turgenev Nietzsche Balzac
Stockton Vatsyayana Crane
Burroughs Verne Vinci
Curtis Tocqueville Gogol Busch
Homer Widger Tolstoy Whitman
Darwin Thoreau Twain Scott Plato Harte
Potter Freud Zola Lawrence Dickens Burton Hesse
Kant Jowett Stevenson
Andersen Descartes Cervantes Voltaire Cooke
Poe Aristotle Wells
Hale James Hastings Irving
Bunner Shakespeare Chambers
Richter Chekhov da Shaw Benedict Alcott
Doré Dante Wodehouse Pushkin
Swift Newton

 tredition®

tredition was established in 2006 by Sandra Latusseck and Soenke Schulz. Based in Hamburg, Germany, tredition offers publishing solutions to authors and publishing houses, combined with world-wide distribution of printed and digital book content. tredition is uniquely positioned to enable authors and publishing houses to create books on their own terms and without conventional manu-facturing risks.

For more information please visit: www.tredition.com

TREDITION CLASSICS

This book is part of the TREDITION CLASSICS series. The creators of this series are united by passion for literature and driven by the intention of making all public domain books available in printed format again - worldwide. Most TREDITION CLASSICS titles have been out of print and off the bookstore shelves for decades. At tredition we believe that a great book never goes out of style and that its value is eternal. Several mostly non-profit literature projects provide content to tredition. To support their good work, tredition donates a portion of the proceeds from each sold copy. As a reader of a TREDITION CLASSICS book, you support our mission to save many of the amazing works of world literature from oblivion. See all available books at www.tredition.com.

Project Gutenberg

The content for this book has been graciously provided by Project Gutenberg. Project Gutenberg is a non-profit organization founded by Michael Hart in 1971 at the University of Illinois. The mission of Project Gutenberg is simple: To encourage the creation and distribu-tion of eBooks. Project Gutenberg is the first and largest collection of public domain eBooks.

Godolphin

Volume 6

Baron Edward Bulwer Lytton Lytton

Imprint

GODOLPHIN, Volume 6.
By Edward Bulwer Lytton
(Lord Lytton)

CHAPTER LIX.

CONSTANCE MAKES A DISCOVERY THAT TOUCHES AND ENLIGHTENS HER AS TO GODOLPHIN'S NATURE. — AN EVENT, ALTHOUGH IN PRIVATE LIFE, NOT WITHOUT ITS INTEREST.

If Constance most bitterly reproached herself, or rather her slackened nerves, her breaking health, that she had before another — that other too, not of her own sex — betrayed her dependence upon even her husband's heart for happiness; if her conscience instantly took alarm at the error (and it was indeed a grave one) which had revealed to any man her domestic griefs; yet, on the other hand, she could not control the wild thrill of delight with which she recalled those words that had so solemnly assured her she was still beloved by Godolphin. She had a firm respect in Radclyffe's penetration and his sincerity, and knew that he was one neither to deceive her nor be deceived himself. His advice, too, came home to her. Had she, indeed, with sufficient address, sufficient softness, insinuated herself into Godolphin's nature? Neglected herself, had she not neglected in return? She asked herself this question, and was never weary of examining her past conduct. That Radclyffe, the austere and chilling Radclyffe, entertained for her any feeling warmer than friendship, she never for an instant suspected; that suspicion alone would have driven him from her presence for ever. And although there had been a time, in his bright and exulting youth, when Radclyffe had not been without those arts which win, in the opposite sex, affection from aversion itself, those arts doubled, ay, a hundredfold, in their fascination, would not have availed him with the pure but disappointed Constance, even had a sense of right and wrong very different from the standard he now acknowledged permitted him to exert them. So that his was rather the sacrifice of impulse, than of any triumph that impulse could afterwards have gained him.

Many, and soft and sweet were now the recollections of Constance. Her heart flew back to her early love among the shades of Wendover; to the first confession of the fair enthusiastic boy, when he offered at her shrine a mind, a genius, a heart capable of fruits which the indolence of after-life, and the lethargy of disappointed hope, had blighted before their time.

If he was now so deaf to what she considered the nobler, because more stirring, excitements of life, was she not in some measure answerable for the supineness? Had there not been a day in which he had vowed to toil, to labour, to sacrifice the very character of his mind, for a union with her? Was she, after all, was she right to adhere so rigidly to her father's dying words, and to that vow afterwards confirmed by her own pride and bitterness of soul? She looked to her father's portrait for an answer; and that daring and eloquent face seemed, for the first time, cold and unanswering to her appeal.

In such meditations the hours passed, and midnight came on without Constance having quitted her apartment. She now summoned her woman, and inquired if Godolphin was at home. He had come in about an hour since, and, complaining of fatigue, had retired to rest. Constance again dismissed her maid, and stole to his apartment. He was already asleep, his cheek rested on his arm, and his hair fell wildly over a brow that now worked under the influence of his dreams. Constance put the light softly down, and seating herself beside him, watched over a sleep which, if it had come suddenly on him, was not the less unquiet and disturbed. At length he muttered, "Yes, Lucilla, yes; I tell you, you are avenged. I have not forgotten you! I have not forgotten that I betrayed, deserted you! but was it my fault? No, no! Yet I have not the less sought to forget it. These poor excesses,—these chilling gaieties,—were they not incurred for you?—and now you come—you—ah, no—spare me!"

Shocked and startled, Constance drew back. Here was a new key to Godolphin's present life, his dissipation, his thirst for pleasure. Had he indeed sought to lull the stings of conscience? And she, instead of soothing, of reconciling him to the past, had she left him alone to struggle with bitter and unresting thoughts, and to contrast the devotion of the one lost with the indifference of the one gained? She crept back to her own chamber, to commune with her heart and be still.

"My dear Percy," said she, the next day, when he carelessly sauntered into her boudoir before he rode out, "I have a favour to ask of you."

"Who ever denied a favour to Lady Erpingham?"

"Not you, certainly; but my favour is a great one."

"It is granted."

"Let us pass the summer in − −shire."

Godolphin's brow clouded.

"At Wendover Castle?" said he, after a pause.

"We have never been there since our marriage," said Constance evasively.

"Humph!−as you will."

"It was the place," said Constance, "where you, Percy, first told me you loved!"

The tone of his wife's voice struck on the right chord in Godolphin's breast; he looked up, and saw her eyes full of tears and fixed upon him.

"Why, Constance," said he, much affected, "who would have thought that you still cherished that remembrance?"

"Ah! when shall I forget it?" said Constance; "then you loved me!"

"And was rejected."

"Hush! but I believe now that I was wrong."

"No, Constance; you were wrong, for your own happiness, that the rejection was not renewed."

"Percy!"

"Constance!" and in the accent of that last word there was something that encouraged Constance, and she threw herself into Godolphin's arms, and murmured:−

"If I have offended, forgive me; let us be to each other what we once were."

Words like these from the lips of one in whom such tender supplications, such feminine yearnings, were not common, subdued Godolphin at once. He folded her in his arms, and kissing her passionately, whispered, "Be always thus, Constance, and you will be more to me than ever."

CHAPTER LX.

THE REFORM BILL.—A VERY SHORT CHAPTER.

This reconcilation was not so short-lived as matters of the kind frequently are. There is a Chinese proverb which says: "How near are two hearts when there is no deceit between them!" And the misunderstanding of their mutual sentiments being removed, their affection became at once visible to each other. And Constance reproaching herself for her former pride mingled in her manner to her husband a gentle, even an humble sweetness, which, being exactly that which he had most desired in her, was what most attracted him.

At this time, Lord John Russell brought forward the Bill of Parliamentary Reform. Lady Erpingham. was in the lantern of the House of Commons on that memorable night; like every one else, her feelings at first were all absorbed in surprise. She went home; she hastened to Godolphin's library. Leaning his head on his hand, that strange person, in the midst of events that stirred the destinies of Europe, was absorbed in the old subtleties of Spinosa. In the frank confidence of revived love, she put her hand upon his shoulder, and told him rapidly that news which was then on its way to terrify or delight the whole of England.

"Will this charm you, dear Constance?" said he kindly; "is it a blow to the party you hate, and I sympathise with — or — —

"My father," interrupted Constance, passionately, "would to Heaven he had seen this day! It was this system, the patron and the nominee system, that crushed, and debased, and killed him. And now, I shall see that system destroyed!"

"So, then, my Constance will go over to the Whigs in earnest?"

"Yes, because I shall meet there truth and the people!"

Godolphin laughed gently at the French exaggeration of the saying, and Constance forgave him. The fine ladies of London were a little divided as to the merits of the "Bill;" Constance was the first that declared in its favour. She was air important ally — as important at least as a woman can be. A bright spirit reigned in her eye; her step grew more elastic; her voice more glad. This was the happiest time of her life — she was happy in the renewal of her love, happy in the approaching triumph of her hate.

CHAPTER LXI.

THE SOLILOQUY OF THE SOOTHSAYER. — AN EPISODICAL MYSTERY, INTRODUCED AS A TYPE OF THE MANY THINGS IN LIFE THAT ARE NEVER ACCOUNTED FOR. — GRATUITOUS DEVIATIONS FROM OUR COMMON CAREER.

In Leicester Square there is a dim old house, which I have but this instant visited, in order to bring back more vividly to my recollection the wild and unhappy being who, for some short time, inhabited its old-fashioned and gloomy chambers.

In that house, at the time I now speak of, lodged the mysterious Liehbur. It was late at noon, and she sat alone in her apartment, which was darkened so as to exclude the broad and peering sun. There was no trick, nor sign of the fallacious art she professed, visible in the large and melancholy room. One or two books in the German language lay on the table beside which she sat: but they were of the recent poetry, and not of the departed dogmas, of the genius of that tongue. The enthusiast was alone; and, with her hand supporting her chin, and her eyes fixed on vacancy, she seemed feeding in silence the thoughts that flitted to and fro athwart a brain which had for years lost its certain guide; a deserted mansion, whence the lord had departed, and where spirits not of this common life had taken up their haunted and desolate abode. And never was there a countenance better suited to the character which this singular woman had assumed. Rich, thick, auburn hair was parted loosely over a brow in which the large and full temples would have betrayed to a phrenologist the great preponderance which the dreaming and the imaginative bore over the sterner faculties. Her eyes were deep, intense, but of the bright and wandering glitter which is so powerful in its effect on the beholder, because it betokens that thought which is not of this daily world and inspires that fear, that sadness, that awe, which few have looked on the face of the insane and not experienced. Her features were still noble, and of the fair Greek symmetry of the painter's Sibyl; but the cheeks were worn and hollow, and one bright spot alone broke their marble paleness; her lips were, however, full, and yet red, and by their uncertain and varying play, gave frequent glimpses of teeth lustrously white; which, while completing the beauty of her face, aided—with somewhat of a fearful effect—the burning light of her strange eyes, and the vague, mystic expression of her abrupt and unjoyous smile. You might see when her features were, as now, in a momentary repose, that her health was broken, and that she was not long sentenced to wander over that world where the soul had already ceased to find its home; but the instant she spoke, her colour deepened, and the brilliant and rapid alternations of her countenance deceived the eye, and concealed the ravages of the worm that preyed within.

"Yes," said she, at last breaking silence, and soliloquising in the English tongue, but with somewhat of a foreign accent; "yes, I am in his city; within a few paces of his home; I have seen him, I have heard him. Night after night—in rain, and in the teeth of the biting winds, I have wandered round his home. Ay! and I could have raised my voice, and shrieked a warning and a prophecy, that should have startled him from his sleep as the trumpet of the last angel! but I hushed the sound within my soul, and covered the vision with a thick silence. O God! what have I seen, and felt, and known, since he last saw me! But we shall meet again; and ere the year has rolled round, I shall feel the touch of his lips and die! Die! what calmness, what luxury in the word! The fiery burthen of this dread knowledge I have heaped upon me, shuffled off; memory no more; the past, the present, the future exorcised; and a long sleep, with bright dreams of a lulling sky, and a silver voice, and his presence!"

The door opened, and a black girl of about ten years old, in the costume of her Moorish tribe, announced the arrival of a new visitor. The countenance of Madame Liehbur changed at once into an expression of cold and settled calmness; she ordered the visitor to be admitted; and presently, Stainforth Radclyffe entered the room.

* * * * * * * * * * *

"Thou mistakest me and my lore," said the diviner; "I meddle not with the tricks and schemes of the worldly; I show the truth, not garble it."

"Pshaw!" said Radclyffe, impatiently; "this jargon cannot deceive me. You exhibit your skill for money. I ask one exertion of it, and desire you to name your reward. Let us talk after the fashion of this world, and leave that of the other to our dupes."

"Yet, thou hast known grief too," said the diviner, musingly, "and those who have sorrowed ought to judge more gently of each other. Wilt thou try my art on thyself, ere thou askest it for others?"

"Ay, if you could restore the dead to my dreams."

"I can!" replied the soothsayer, sternly.

Radclyffe laughed bitterly. "Away with this talk to me; or, if you would convince me, raise at once the spectre I desire to see!"

"And dost thou think, vain man," replied Liehbur, haughtily, "that I pretend to the power thou speakest of? Yes; but not as the impostors of old (dull and gross, appealing to outward spells, and spells wrought by themselves alone) affected to do. I can bring the dead before thee, but thou thyself must act upon thyself."

"Mummery! What would you drive at?"

"Wilt thou fast three days, and for three nights abstain from sleep, and then visit me once again?"

"No, fair deluder; such a preliminary is too much to ask of a Neophyte. Three days without food, and three nights without sleep! Why, you would have to raise myself from the dead!"

"And canst thou," said the diviner, with great dignity, "canst thou hope that thou wouldst be worthy of a revelation from a higher world—that for thee the keys of the grave should unlock their awful treasure, and the dead return to life, when thou scruplest to mortify thy flesh and. loosen the earthly bonds that cumber and chain the spirit? I tell thee, that only as the soul detaches itself from the frame, can its inner and purer sense awaken, and the full consciousness of the invisible and divine things that surround it descend upon its powers."

"And what," said Radclyffe, startled more by the countenance and voice than the words themselves of the soothsayer; "what would you then do, supposing that I perform this penance?"

"Awaken to their utmost sense, even to pain and torture, the naked nerves of that Great Power thou callest the Imagination; that Power which presides over dreams and visions, which kindles song, and lives in the heart of Melodies; which inspired the Magian of the East and the Pythian voices—and, in the storms and thunder of savage lands originated the notion of a God and the seeds of human worship; that vast presiding Power which, to the things of mind, is what the Deity is to the Universe itself—the creator of all. I would awaken, I say, that Power from its customary sleep where, buried in the heart, it folds its wings, and lives but by fits and starts, unquiet, but unaroused; and by that Power thou wouldst see, and feel, and know, and through it only thou wouldst exist. So that it would be with thee, as if the body were not: as if thou wert already all-spiritual, all-living. So thou wouldst learn in life that which may be open to thee after death; and so, soul might now, as hereafter, converse with soul, and revoke the Past, and sail prescient down the dark tides of the Future. A brief and fleeting privilege, but dearly purchased: be wise, and disbelieve in it; be happy, and reject it!"

Radclyffe was impressed, despite himself, by the solemn novelty of this language, and the deep mournfulness with which the soothsayer's last sentence died away.

"And how," said he, after a pause, "how, and by what arts would you so awaken the imaginative faculty?"

"Ask not until the time comes for the trial," answered Liebhur.

"But can you awaken it in all?—the dull, the unideal, as in the musing and exalted?"

"No! but the dull and unideal will not go through the necessary ordeal. Few besides those for whom fate casts her great parts in life's drama, ever come to that point when I can teach them the Future."

"Do you mean that your chief votaries are among the great? Pardon me, I should have thought the most superstitious are to be found among the most ignorant and lowly."

"Yes; but they consult only what imposes on their credulity, without demanding stern and severe sacrifice of time and enjoyment, as I do. The daring, the resolute, the scheming with their souls intent upon great objects and high dreams-those are the men who despise the charms of the moment, who are covetous of piercing the far future, who know how much of their hitherward career has been brightened, not by genius or nature, but some strange confluence of events, some mysterious agency of fate. The great are always fortunate, and therefore mostly seekers into the decrees of fortune."

So great is the influence which enthusiasm, right or wrong, always exercises over us, that even the hard and acute Radclyffe-who had entered the room with the most profound contempt for the pretensions of the soothsayer, and partly from a wish to find materials for ridiculing a folly of the day, partly, it may be from the desire to examine which belonged to his nature—began to consider in his own mind whether he should yield to his curiosity, now strongly excited, and pledge himself to the preliminary penance the diviner had ordained.

The soothsayer continued:—

"The stars, and the clime, and the changing moon have power over us—why not? Do they not have influence over the rest of nature? But we can only unravel their more august and hidden secrets, by giving full wing to the creative spirit which first taught us their elementary nature, and which, when released from earth, will have full range to wander over their brilliant fields. Know in one word, the Imagination and the Soul are one, one indivisible and the same; on that truth rests all my lore."

"And if I followed your precepts, what other preliminaries would you enjoin?"

"Not until thou engagest to perform them, will I tell thee more."

"I engage!"

"And swear?"

"I swear!"

The soothsayer rose — and — —

* * * * * * * * * * * * * *

CHAPTER LXII.

IN WHICH THE COMMON LIFE GLIDES INTO THE STRANGE. — EQUALLY TRUE, BUT THE TRUTH NOT EQUALLY ACKNOWLEDGED.

It was on the night of this interview that Constance, coming into Godolphin's room, found him leaning against the wall, pale, and agitated, and almost insensible. "Percy — Percy, you are ill!" she exclaimed, and wound her arms round his neck. He looked at her long and wistfully, breathing hard all the time, until at length he seemed slowly to recover his self-possession, and seating himself, motioned Constance to do the same. After a pause, he said, clasping her hand.

"Listen to me, Constance. My health, I fear, is breaking; I am tormented by fearful visions; I am possessed by some magic influence. For several nights successively, before falling asleep, a cold tremor has gradually pervaded my frame; the roots of my hair stand on end; my teeth chatter; a vague horror seizes me; my blood seems turned to a solid substance, so curdled and stagnant is it. I strive to speak, to cry out, but my voice clings to the roof of my mouth; I feel that I have no longer power over myself. Suddenly, and in the very midst of this agony, I fall into a heavy sleep; then come strange bewildering dreams, with Volktman's daughter for ever presiding over them; but with a changed countenance, calm, unutterably calm, and gazing on me with eyes that burn into my soul. The dream fades, I wake with the morning, but exhausted and enfeebled. I have consulted physicians; I have taken drugs; but I cannot break the spell — the previous horror and the after-dreams. And just now, Constance, just now — you see the window is open to the park, the gate of the garden is unclosed; I happened to lift my eyes, and lo! gazing upon me in the sickly moonlight, was the countenance of my dreams — Lucilla's, but how altered! Merciful Heaven! is it a mockery, or can the living Lucilla really be in England? and have these visions, these terrors been part of that mysterious sympathy which united us ever, and which her father predicted should cease but with our lives?"

The emotions of Godolphin were so rarely visible, and in the present instance they were so unaffected, and so roused, that Constance could not summon courage to soothe, to cheer him; she herself was alarmed and shocked, and glanced fearfully towards the window, lest the apparition he had spoken of should reappear. All without was still, not a leaf stirred on the trees in the Mall; no human figure was to be seen. She turned again to Godolphin, and kissed the drops from his brow, and pressed his cheek to her bosom.

"I have a presentiment," said he, "that something dreadful will happen shortly. I feel as if I were near some great crisis of my life; and as if I were about to step from the bright and palpable world into regions of cloud and dark ness. Constance, strange misgivings as to my choice in my past life haunt and perplex me. I have sought only the present; I have adjured all toil, all ambition, and laughed at the future; my hand has plucked the rose-leaves, and now they lie withered in the grasp. My youth flies me—age scowls on me from the distance; an age of frivolities that I once scorned; yet—yet, had I formed a different creed, how much I might have done! But—but, out on this cant! My nerves are shattered, and I prate nonsense. Lend me your arm, Constance, let us go into the saloon, and send for music!"

And all that night Constance watched by the side of Godolphin, and marked in mute terror the convulsions that wrung his sleep, the foam that gathered to his lip, the cries that broke from his tongue. But she was rewarded when, with the grey dawn, he awoke, and, catching her tender and tearful gaze, flung himself upon her bosom, and bade God bless her for her love!

CHAPTER LXIII.

**A MEETING BETWEEN CONSTANCE AND THE PROPHET-
ESS.**

A strange suspicion had entered Constance's mind, and for Godolphin's sake she resolved to put it to the proof. She drew her mantle round her stately figure, put on a large disguising bonnet, and repaired to Madame Liehbur's house.

The Moorish girl opened the door to the countess; and her strange dress, her African hue and features, relieved by the long, glittering pendants in her ears, while they seemed suited to the eccentric reputation of her mistress, brought a slight smile to the proud lip of Lady Erpingham, as she conceived them a part of the charlatanism practised by the soothsayer. The girl only replied to Lady Erpingham's question by an intelligent sign; and running lightly up the stairs, conducted the guest into an anteroom, where she waited but for a few moments before she was admitted into Madame Liehbur's apartment.

The effect that the personal beauty of the diviner always produced on those who beheld her was not less powerful than usual on the surprised and admiring gaze of Lady Erpingham. She bowed her haughty brow with involuntary respect, and took the seat to which the enthusiast beckoned.

"And what, lady," said the soothsayer, in the foreign music of her low voice, "what brings thee hither? Wouldst thou gain, or hast thou lost, that gift our poor sex prizes so dearly beyond its value? Is it of love that thou wouldst speak to the interpreter of dreams and the priestess of the things to come?"

While the bright-eyed Liehbur thus spoke, the countess examined through her veil the fair face before her, comparing it with that description which Godolphin had given her of the sculptor's daughter, and her suspicion acquired new strength.

"I seek not that which you allude to," said Constance; "but of the future, although without any definite object, I would indeed like to question you. All of us love to pry into dark recesses hid from our view, and over which you profess the empire."

"Your voice is sweet, but commanding," said the oracle; and your air is stately, as of one born in courts. Lift your veil, that I may gaze upon your face, and tell by its lines the fate your character has shaped for you."

"Alas!" answered Constance, "life betrays few of its past signs by outward token. If you have no wiser art than that drawn from the lines and features of our countenances, I shall still remain what I am now — an unbeliever in your powers."

"The brow, and the lip, and the eye, and the expression of each and all," answered Liehbur, "are not the lying index you suppose them."

"Then," rejoined Constance, "by those signs will I read your own destiny, as you would read mine."

The sibyl started, and waved her hand impatiently; but Constance proceeded.

"Your birth, despite your fair locks, was under a southern sky; you were nursed in the delusions you now teach; you were loved, and left alone; you are in the country of your lover. Is it not so? — am I not an oracle in my turn?"

The mysterious Liehbur fell back in her chair; her lips apart and blanched — her hands clasped — her eyes fixed upon her visitant.

"Who are you?" she cried at last, in a shrill tone; "who, of my own sex, knows my wretched history? Speak, speak! — in mercy speak! tell me more! convince me that you have but vainly guessed my secret, or that you have a right to know it!"

"Did not your father forsake, for the blue skies of Rome, his own colder shores?" continued Constance, adopting the heightened and romantic tone of the one she addressed; and, "Percy Godolphin — is that name still familiar to the ear of Lucilla Volktman?"

A loud, long shriek burst from the lips of the soothsayer, and she sank at once lifeless on the ground. Greatly alarmed, and repenting her own abruptness, Constance hastened to her assistance. She lifted the poor being, whom she unconsciously had once contributed so deeply to injure, from the ground; she loosened her dress, and perceived that around her neck hung a broad ivory necklace wrought with curious characters, and many uncouth forms and symbols. This evidence that, in deluding others, the soothsayer deluded herself also, touched and affected the countess; and while she was still busy in chafing the temples of Lucilla, the Moor, brought to the spot by that sudden shriek, entered the apartment. She seemed surprised and terrified at her mistress's condition, and poured forth, in some tongue unknown to Constance, what seemed to her a volley of mingled reproach and lamentation. She seized Lady Erpingham's hand, dashed it indignantly away, and, supporting herself the ashen cheek of Lucilla, motioned to Lady Erpingham to depart; but Constance, not easily accustomed to obey, retained her position beside the still insensible Lucilla; and now, by slow degrees, and with quick and heavy sighs, the unfortunate daughter of Volktman returned to life and consciousness.

In assisting Lucilla, the countess had thrown aside her veil, and the eyes of the soothsayer opened upon that superb beauty, which once to see was never to forget. Involuntarily she again closed her eyes, and groaned audibly; and then, summoning all her courage, she withdrew her hand from Constance's clasp, and bade her Moorish handmaid leave them once more alone.

"So, then," said Lucilla, after a pause, "it is Percy Godolphin's wife; his English wife, who has come to gaze on the fallen, the degraded Lucilla; and yet," sinking her voice into a tone of ineffable and plaintive sweetness—"yet I have slept on his bosom, and been dear and sacred to him as thou! Go, proud lady, go!—leave me to my mad, and sunken, and solitary state. Go!"

"Dear Lucilla!" said Constance, kindly, and striving once more to take her hand, "do not cast me away from you. I have long sympathised with your generous although erring heart—your bard and bitter misfortunes. Look on me only as your friend—nay, your sister, if you will. Let me persuade you to leave this strange and desultory life; choose your own home: I am rich to overflowing; all you can desire shall be at your command. He shall not know more of you unless (to assuage the remorse that the memory of you does, I know, still occasion him) you will suffer him to learn, from your own hand, that you are well and at ease, and that you do not revoke your former pardon. Come, dear Lucilla!" and the arm of the generous and bright-souled Constance gently wound round the feeble frame of Lucilla, who now, reclining back, wept as if her heart would break.

"Come, give me the deep, the grateful joy of thinking I can minister to your future comforts. I was the cause of all your wretchedness; but for me, Godolphin would have been yours for ever—would probably, by marriage, have redressed your wrongs; but for me you would not have wandered an outcast over the inhospitable world. Let me in something repair what I have cost you. Speak to me, Lucilla!"

"Yes, I will speak to you," said poor Lucilla, throwing herself on the ground, and clasping with grateful warmth the knees of her gentle soother; "for long, long years—I dare not think how many—I have not heard the voice of kindness fall upon my ear. Among strange faces and harsh tongues hath my lot been cast; and if I have wrought out from the dreams of my young hours the course of this life (which you contemn, but not justly), it has been that I may stand alone and not dependent; feared and not despised. And now you, you whom I admire and envy, and would reverence more than living woman (for he loves you and deems you worthy of him), you, lady, speak to me as a sister would speak, and—and— —" Here sobs interrupted Lucilla's speech; and Constance herself, almost equally affected, and finding it vain to attempt to raise her, knelt by her side, and tenderly caressing her, sought to comfort her, even while she wept in doing so.

And this was a beautiful passage in the life of the lofty Constance. Never did she seem more noble than when, thus lowly and humbling herself, she knelt beside the poor victim of her husband's love, and whispered to the diseased and withering heart tidings of comfort, charity, home, and a futurity of honour and of peace. But this was not a dream that could long lull the perturbed and erring brain of Lucilla Volktman. And when she recovered, in some measure, her self-possession, she rose, and throwing back the wild hair from her throbbing temples, she said, in a calm and mournful voice:

"Your kindness comes too late. I am dying, fast—fast. All that is left to me in the world are these very visions, this very power—call it delusion if you will—from which you would tear me. Nay, look not so reproachfully, and in such wonder. Do you not know that men have in poverty, sickness, and all outer despair, clung to a creative spirit within—a world peopled with delusions—and called it Poetry? and that gift has been more precious to them than all that wealth and pomp could bestow? So," continued Lucilla, with fervid and insane enthusiasm, "so is this, my creative spirit, my imaginary world, my inspiration, what poetry may be to others. I may be mistaken in the truth of my belief. There are times when my brain is cool, and my frame at rest, and I sit alone and think over the real past—when I feel my trust shaken, and my ardour damped: but that thought does not console but torture me, and I hasten to plunge once more among the charms, and spells, and mighty dreams, that wrap me from my living self. Oh, lady! bright, and beautiful, and lofty, as you are, there may come a time when you can conceive that even madness may be a relief. For" (and here the wandering light burned brighter in the enthusiast's glowing eyes), "for, when the night is round us, and there is peace on earth, and the world's children sleep, it is a wild joy to sit alone and vigilant, and forget that we live and are wretched. The stars speak to us then with a wondrous and stirring voice; they tell us of the doom of men and the wreck of empires, and prophesy of the far events which they taught to the old Chaldeans. And then the Winds, walking to and fro as they list, bid us go forth with them and hear the songs of the midnight spirits; for you know," she whispered with a smile, putting her hand upon the arm of the appalled and shrinking Constance, who now saw how hopeless was the ministry she had undertaken, "though this world is given up to two tribes of things that live and have a soul: the one bodily and palpable as we are; the other more glorious, but invisible to our dull sight—though I have seen them— Dread Solemn Shadows, even in their mirth; the night is their season as the day is ours; they march in the moonbeams, and are borne upon the wings of the winds. And with them, and by their thoughts, I raise myself from what I am and have been. Ah, lady, wouldst thou take this comfort from me?"

"But," said Constance, gathering courage from the gentleness which Lucilla's insanity now wore, and trying to soothe, not contradict her in her present vein, "but in the country, Lucilla, in some quiet and sheltered nook, you might indulge these visions without the cares and uncertainty that must now perplex you; without leading this dangerous and roving life, which must at times expose you to insult, to annoyance, and discontent you with, yourself."

"You are mistaken, lady," said the astrologer, proudly; "none know me who do not fear. I am powerful, and I hug my power — it comforts me: without it, what should I be? — an abject, forsaken, miserable woman. No! that power I possess — to shake men's secret souls — even if it be a deceit — even if I should laugh at them, not pity — reconciles me to myself and to the past. And I am not poor, madam," as, with the common caprice of her infirmity, an angry suspicion seemed to cross her; "I want no one's charity, I have learned to maintain myself. Nay, I could be even wealthy if I would!"

"And," said Constance, seeing that for the present she must postpone her benevolent intentions, "and he — Godolphin — you forgive him still?"

At that name, it was as if a sudden charm had been whispered to the fevered heart of the poor fanatic; her head sank from its proud bearing; a deep, a soft blush coloured the wan cheek; her arms drooped beside her; she trembled violently; and, after a moment's silence, sank again on her seat and covered her face with her hands. "Ah!" said she, softly, "that word brings me back to my young days, when I asked no power but what love gave me over one heart: it brings me back to the blue Italian lake, and the waving pines, and our solitary home, and my babe's distant grave. Tell me," she cried, again starting up, "has he not spoken of me lately — has he not seen me in his dreams? have I not been present to his soul when the frame, torpid and locked, severed us no more, and, in the still hours, I charmed myself to his gaze? Tell me, has he not owned that Lucilla haunted his pillow? Tell me; and if I err, my spells are nothing, my power is vanity, and I am the helpless creature thou wouldst believe me!"

Despite her reason and her firm sense, Constance half shuddered at these mysterious words, as she recalled what Percy had told her of his dreams the preceding evening, and the emotions she herself had witnessed in his slumbers when she watched beside his bed. She remained silent, and Lucilla regarded her countenance with a sort of triumph.

"My art, then, is not so idle as thou wouldst hold it. But—hush!—last night I beheld him, not in spirit, but visibly, face to face: for I wander at times before his home (his home was once mine!) and he saw me, and was smitten with fear; in these worn features he could recognise not the living Lucilla he had known. But go to him!—thou, his wife, his own—go to him; tell him—no, tell him not of me. He must not seek me; we must not held parley together: for oh, lady" (and Lucilla's face became settled into an expression so sad, so unearthly sad, that no word can paint, no heart conceive, its utter and solemn sorrow), "when we two meet again to commune,—to converse,—when once more I touch that band, when once more I feel that beloved, that balmy breath;—my last hour is at hand—and danger—imminent, dark, and deadly danger, clings fast to him!"

As she spoke, Lucilla closed her eyes, as it to shut some horrid vision from her gaze; and Constance looked fearfully round, almost expecting some apparition at hand. Presently Lucilla, moving silently across the room, beckoned to the countess to follow: she did so: they entered another apartment: before a recess there hung a black curtain: Lucilla drew it slowly aside, and Constance turned her eyes from a dazzling light that broke upon them; when she again looked, she beheld a sort of glass dial marked with various quaint hieroglyphics and the figures of angels, beautifully wrought; but around the dial, which was circular, were ranged many stars, and the planets, set in due order. These were lighted from within by some chemical process, and burnt with a clear and lustrous, but silver light. And Constance observed that the dial turned round, and that the stars turned with it, each in a separate motion; and in the midst of the dial were the bands as of a clock-that moved, but so slowly, that the most patient gaze alone could observe the motion.

While the wondering Constance regarded this singular device, Lucilla pointed to one star that burned brighter than the rest; and below it, half-way down the dial, was another, a faint and sickly orb, that, when watched, seemed to perform a much more rapid and irregular course than its fellows.

"The bright star is his," said she; "and yon dim and dying one is the type of mine. Note: in the course they both pursue they must meet at last; and when they meet, the mechanism of the whole halts—the work of the dial is for ever done. These hands indicate hourly the progress made to that end; for it is the mimicry and symbol of mine. Thus do I number the days of my fate; thus do I know, even almost to a second, the period in which I shall join my Father that is in Heaven!

"And now," continued the maniac (though maniac is too harsh and decided a word for the dreaming wildness of Lucilla's insanity), as, dropping the curtain, she took her guest's hand and conducted her back into the outer room—"and now, farewell! You sought me, and, I feel, only from kind and generous motives. We never shall meet more. Tell not your husband that you have seen me. He will know soon, too soon, of my existence: fain would I spare him that pang and," growing pale as she spoke, "that peril; but Fate forbids it. What is writ, is writ: and who shall blot God's sentence from the stars, which are His book? Farewell! high thoughts are graved upon your brow may they bless you; or, where they fail to bless, may they console and support. Farewell! I have not yet forgotten to be grateful, and I still dare to pray."

Thus saying, Lucilla kissed the hand she had held, and turning hastily away, regained the room she had just left; and, locking the door, left the stunned and bewildered countess to depart from the melancholy abode. With faltering steps she quitted the chamber, and at the foot of the stairs the little Moor awaited her. To her excited fancy there was something eltrich and preternatural in the gaze of the young African, and the grin of her pearly teeth, as she opened the door to the visitant. Hastening to her carriage, which she had left at a corner of the square, the countess rejoiced when she gained it; and throwing herself back on the luxurious cushions, felt as exhausted by this starry and weird incident in the epic of life's common career, as if she had partaken of that overpowering inspiration which she now almost incredulously asked herself, as she looked forth on the broad day and the busy streets, if she had really witnessed.

CHAPTER LXIV.

LUCILLA'S FLIGHT. — THE PERPLEXITY OF LADY ERPING-HAM. — A CHANGE COMES OVER GODOLPHIN'S MIND. — HIS CONVERSATION WITH RADCLYFFE. — GENERAL ELEC-TION. — GODOLPHIN BECOMES A SENATOR.

No human heart ever beat with more pure and generous emotions, when freed from the political fever that burned within her (withering, for the moment, the chastened and wholesome impulses of her nature), than those which animated the heart of the queenly Constance. She sent that evening for the most celebrated physician in London — that polished and courtly man who seems born for the maladies of the drawing-room, but who beneath so urbane a demeanour, conceals so accurate and profound a knowledge of the disorders of his unfortunate race. I say accurate and profound comparatively, for positive knowledge of pathology is what no physician in modern times and civilized countries really possesses. No man cures us — the highest art is not to kill! Constance, then, sent for this physician, and, as delicately as possible, related the unfortunate state of Lucilla, and the deep anxiety she felt for her mental and bodily relief. The physician promised to call the next day; he did so, late in the afternoon — Lucilla was gone. Strange, self-willed, mysterious, she came like a dream, to warn, to terrify, and to depart. They knew not whither she had fled, and her Moorish handmaid alone attended her.

Constance was deeply chagrined at this intelligence; for she had already begun to build castles in the air, which poor Lucilla, with a frame restored, and a heart at ease, and nothing left of the past but a soft and holy penitence, should inhabit. The countess, however, consoled herself with the hope that Lucilla would at least write to her, and mention her new place of residence; but days passed and no letter came.

Constance felt that her benevolent intentions were doomed to be unfulfilled. She was now greatly perplexed whether or not to relate to Godolphin the interview that had taken place between her and

Lucilla. She knew the deep, morbid, and painful interest which the memory of this wild and visionary creature created in Godolphin; and she trembled at the feeling she might re-awaken by even a faint picture of the condition and mental infirmities of her whose life he had so darkly shadowed. She resolved, therefore, at all events for the present, and until every hope of discovering Lucilla once more had expired, to conceal the meeting that had occurred. And in this resolve she was strengthened by perceiving that Godolphin's mind had become gradually calmed from its late excitement, and that he had begun to consider, or at least appeared to consider the apparition of Lucilla at his window, as the mere delusion of a heated imagination. His nights grew once more tranquil, and freed from the dark dreams that had tormented his brain; and even the cool and unimaginative Constance could scarcely divest herself of the wild fancy that, when Lucilla was near, a secret and preternatural sympathy between Godolphin and the reader of the stars had produced that influence over his nightly dreams which paled, and receded, and vanished, as Lucilla departed from the actual circle in which he lived.

It was at this time, too, that a change was perceptible in Godolphin's habits, and crept gradually over the character of his thoughts. Dissipation ceased to allure him, the light wit of his parasites palled upon his ear; magnificence had lost its gloss, and the same fastidious, exacting thirst for the ideal which had disappointed him in the better objects of life, began now to discontent him with its glittering pleasures.

The change was natural and the causes not difficult to fathom. The fact was, that Godolphin had now arrrived at that period of existence when a man's character is almost invariably subject to great change; the crisis in life's fever, when there is a new turn in our fate, and our moral death or regeneration is sealed by the silent wavering, or the solemn decision of the Hour. Arrived at the confines of middle age, there is an outward innovation in the whole system; unlooked-for symptoms break forth in the bodily, unlooked-for symptoms in the mental, frame. It happened to Godolphin that, at this critical period, a chance, a circumstance, a straw, had reunited his long interrupted, but never stifled affections to the image of his beautiful Constance. The reign of passion, the magic of those sweet illusions, that ineffable yearning which possession mocks, although it quells at last, were indeed for ever over; but a friendship more soft and genial than exists in any relation, save that of husband and wife, had sprung up, almost as by a miracle (so sudden was it), between breasts for years divided. And the experience of those years had taught Godolphin how frail and unsubstantial had been all the other ties he had formed. He wondered, as sitting alone with Constance, her tenderness recalled the past, her wit enlivened the present, and his imagination still shed a glory and a loveliness over the future, that he had been so long insensible to the blessing of that communion which he now experienced. He did not perceive what in fact was the case—that the tastes and sympathies of each, blunted by that disappointment which is the child of experience, were more willing to concede somewhat to the tastes and sympathies of the other; that Constance gave a more indulgent listening to his beautiful refinements of an ideal and false epicurism; that he, smiling still, smiled with kindness, not with scorn, at the sanguine politics, the worldly schemes, and the rankling memories of the intriguing Constance. Fortunately, too, for her, the times were such, that men who never before dreamed of political interference were roused and urged into the mighty conflux of battling interests, which left few moderate and none neuter. Every coterie resounded with political war-cries; every dinner rang; from soup to the coffee, with the merits of the bill; wherever Godolphin turned for refuge, Reform still assailed him; and by degrees the universal feeling, that was at first ridiculed, was at last, although reluctantly, admitted by his mind.

"Why," said he, one clay, musingly, to Radclyffe, whom he met in the old Green Park,—(for since the conversation recorded between Radclyffe and Constance the former came little to Erpingham House), "why should I not try a yet untried experiment? Why should I not live like others in their graver as in their lighter pursuits? I confess, when I look back to the years I have spent in England, I feel that I calculated erroneously. I chalked out a plan—I have followed it rigidly. I have lived for self, for pleasure, for luxury; I have summoned wit, beauty, even wisdom around me. I have been the creator of a magic circle, but to the magician himself the magic was tame and ignoble. In short, I have dreamed, and am awake. Yet, what course of life should supply this, which I think of deserting? Shall I go once more abroad, and penetrate some untravelled corner of the earth? Shall I retire into the country, and write, draining my mind of the excitement that presses on it; or lastly, shall I plunge with my contemporaries into the great gulf of actual events, and strive, and fret, and struggle? — or — in short, Radclyffe, you are a wise man: advise me!"

"Alas!" answered Radclyffe, "it is of no use advising one to be happy who has no object beyond himself. Either enthusiasm, or utter mechanical coldness, is necessary to reconcile men to the cares and mortifications of life. You must feel nothing, or you must feel for others. Unite yourself to a great object; see its goal distinctly; cling to its course courageously; hope for its triumph sanguinely; and on its majestic progress you sail, as in a ship, agitated indeed by the storms, but unheeding the breeze and the surge that would appal the individual effort. The larger public objects make us glide smoothly and unfelt over our minor private griefs. To be happy, my dear Godolphin, you must forget yourself. Your refining and poetical temperament preys upon your content. Learn benevolence — it is the only cure to a morbid nature."

Godolphin was greatly struck by this answer of Radclyffe; the more so, as he had a deep faith in the unaffected sincerity and the calculating wisdom of his adviser. He looked hard in Radclyffe's face, and, after a pause of some moments, replied slowly, "I believe you are right after all; and I have learned in a few short sentences the secret of a discontented life."

Godolphin would have sought other opportunities of conversing with Radclyffe, but events soon parted them. Parliament was dissolved! What an historical event is recorded in those words! The moment the king consented to that measure, the whole series of subsequent events became, to an ordinary prescience, clear as in a mirror. Parliament dissolved in the heat of the popular enthusiasm, a majority, a great majority of Reformers was sure to be returned.

Constance perceived at a glance the whole train of consequences issuing from that one event; perceived and exulted. A glory had gone for ever from the party she abhorred. Her father was already

avenged. She heard his scornful laugh ring forth from the depths of
his forgotten grave.

London emptied itself at once. England was one election. Godolphin remained almost alone. For the first time a sense of littleness
crept over him; a feeling of insignificance, which wounded and
galled his vain nature. In these beat struggles he was nothing. The
admired — the cultivated — spirituel — the splendid Godolphin, sank
below the commonest adventurer, the coarsest brawler — yea, the
humblest freeman, who felt his stake in the state, joined the canvass,
swelled the cry, and helped in the mighty battle between old things
and new, which was so resolutely begun. This feeling gave an impe-
tus to the growth of the new aspirations he had already suffered his
mind to generate; and Constance marked, with vivid delight, that
he now listened to her plans with interest, and examined the political field with a curious and searching gaze.

But she was soon condemned to a disappointment proportioned
to her delight. Though Godolphin had hitherto taken no interest in
party politics, his prejudices, his feelings, his habits of mind, were
all the reverse of democratic. When he once began to examine the
bearings of the momentous question that agitated England, he was
not slow in coming to conclusions which threatened to produce a
permanent disagreement between Constance and himself.

"You wish me to enter Parliament, my dear Constance," said he,
with his quiet smile; "it would be an experiment dangerous to the
union re-established between us. I should vote against your Bill."

"You!" exclaimed Constance, with warmth; "is it possible that you
can sympathise with the fears of a selfish oligarchy — with the cause
of the merchants and traffickers of the plainest right of a free people — the right to select their representatives?"

"My dear Constance," returned Godolphin, "my whole theory of
Government is aristocratic. The right of the, people to choose representatives! — you may as well say the right of the people to choose
kings, or magistrates, and judges — or clergymen and archbishops!
The people have, it is true, the abstract and original right to choose
all these, and every year to chop and change them as they please,
but the people, very properly, in all states, mortgage their lementary
rights for one catholic and practical right — the right to be well gov-

erned. It may be no more to the advantage of the state that the People (that is, the majority, the populace) should elect uncontrolled all the members of the House of Commons—than that they should elect all the pastors of their religion. The sole thing we have to consider is, will they be better governed?"

"Unquestionably," said Constance.

"Unquestionably!—Well, I question it. I foresee a more even balance of parties—nothing else. When parties are evenly balanced states tremble. In good government there should be somewhere sufficient power to carry on, not unexamined, but at least with vigour, the different operations of government itself. In free countries, therefore, one party ought to preponderate sufficiently over the other. If it do not—all the state measures are crippled, delayed, distorted, and the state languishes while the doctors dispute as to the medicines to be applied to it. You will find by your Bill, not that the Tories are destroyed, but that the Whigs and the Radicals are strengthened—the Lords are not crushed—but the Commons are in a state to contest with them. Hence party battles upon catchwords—struggles between the two chambers for things of straw. You who desire progress and movement will find the real affairs of this great Artificial Empire, in its trade—commerce—colonies—internal legislation—standing still while the Whigs and the Tories pelt each other with the quibbles of faction. No I should vote against your Bill! I am not for popular governments, though I like free states. All the advantages of democracy seem to me more than counterbalanced by the sacrifice of the peace and tranquillity, the comfort and the grace, the dignity and the charities of life that democracies usually entail. If the object of men is to live happily—not to strive and to fret—not to make money in the marketplace, and call each other rogues on the hustings, who would not rather be a German than an American? I own I regret to differ from you. For—but no matter——"

"For!—what were you about to say?"

"For—then, since you must know it—I am beginning to feel interest in these questions—excitement is contagious. And after all, if a man really deem his mother-country in some danger, inaction is not philosophy, but a species of parricide. But to think of the daily and hourly pain I should occasion to you, my beloved and ardent Constanceby shocking all your opinions, counteracting all your schemes, working against objects which your father's fate and your early associations have so singularly made duties in your eyes-to do all this is a patriotism beyond me. Let us glide out of this whirlpool, and hoist sail for some nook in the country where we can hear gentler sounds than the roar of the democracy."

Constance sighed, and suffered Godolphin to quit her in silence. But her generous heart was touched by his own generosity. This is one of the great curses of a woman who aspires to the man's part of political controversy. If the man choose to act, the woman, with all her wiles, her intrigues, her arts, is powerless. If Godolphin were to enter Parliament a Tory, the great Whig rendezvous of Erpingham House was lost, and Constance herself a cipher—and her father's wrongs forgotten, and the stern purpose of her masculine career baffled at the very moment of success. She now repented that she had ever desired to draw Godolphin's attention to political matters. She wondered at her own want of foresight. How, with his love for antiquity—his predilections for the elegant and the serene—his philosophy of the "Rose-garden"—could she ever have supposed that he would side with the bold objects and turbulent will of a popular party in a stormy crisis?

The subject was not renewed. But she had the pain of observing that Godolphin's manner was altered: he took pleasure in none of his old hobbies—he was evidently dissatisfied with himself. In fact, it is true that he, for the first time in his life, felt that there is a remorse to the mind as well as to the soul, and that a man of genius cannot be perpetually idle without, as he touches on the middle of his career, looking to the past with some shame, and to the fixture with some ambition. One evening, when he had sat by the open window in a thoughtful and melancholy, almost morose, silence for a considerable time, Constance, after a violent struggle with herself, rose suddenly, and fell on his neck—

"Forgive me, Percy," she said, unable to suppress her tears— "forgive me—it is past—I have no right that you, so superior to myself, should be sacrificed to my—my prejudices you would call them—so be it. Is it for your wife to condemn you to be inglorious?

No—no—dear Godolphin—fulfil your destiny—you are born for high objects. Be active—be distinguished—and I will ask no more!"

John Vernon, in that hour you were forgotten! Who among the dead can ever hope for fidelity, when love to the living invites a woman to betray?

"My sweet Constance," said Godolphin, drawing her to his heart, and affected in proportion as he appreciated all that in that speech his wife gave up for his sake—the all, far more than the lovely person, the splendid wealth, the lofty rank that she had brought to his home—"my sweet Constance, do not think I will take advantage of words so generously, but hastily spoken. Time enough hereafter to think of differences between us. At present let us indulge only the luxury of the new love—the holiness of the new nuptials—that have made us as one Being. Perhaps this restlessness, so unusual to me, will pass away—let us wait awhile. At present 'Sparta has many a worthier son.' One other year, one sweet summer, of the private life we have too much suffered to glide away, enjoyed, and then we will see whether the harsh realities of Ambition be worth either a concession or a dispute. Let us go into the country—to-morrow if you will."

And as Constance was about to answer, he sealed her lips with his kiss.

But Lady Erpingham was not one of those who waver in what they deem a duty. She passed the night in stern and sleepless commune with herself; she was aware of all that she hazarded—all that she renounced: she was even tortured by scruples as to the strange oath that had almost unsexed her. Still, in spite of all, she felt that nothing would excuse her in suffering that gifted and happy intellect, now awakened from the sleep of the Sybarite, to fall back into its lazy and effeminate repose. She had no right to doom a human soul to rot away in its clay. Perhaps, too, she hoped, as all polemical enthusiasts do, that Godolphin, once aroused, would soon become her convert. Be that as it may, she delayed, on various pretences, their departure from London. She went secretly the next day to one of the proprietors of the close Boroughs, the existence of which was about to be annihilated, and a few days afterwards Godolphin received a letter informing him that he had been duly elected member for — —. I will not say what were his feelings at these tidings. Perhaps, such is man's proud and wayward heart, he felt shame to be so outdone by Constance.

CHAPTER LXV.

NEW VIEWS OF A PRIVILEGED ORDER. — THE DEATH-BED OF AUGUSTUS SAVILLE.

This event might indeed have been an era in the life of Percy Godolphin, had that life been spared to a more extended limit than it was; and yet, so long had his ambition been smoothed and polished away by his peculiarities of thought, and so little was his calm and indifferent tone of mind suited to the hot contests and nightly warfare of parliamentary politics, that it is not probable he would ever have won a continuous and solid distinction in a career which requires either obtuseness of mind or enthusiasm of purpose to encounter the repeated mortifications and failures which the most brilliant debutant ordinarily endures. As it was, however, it produced a grave and solemn train of thought in Godolphin's breast. He mused much over his past life, and the musing did not satisfy him. He felt like one of those recorded in physiological history who have been in a trance for years: and now slowly awakening, he acknowledged the stir and rush of revived but confused emotions. Nature, perhaps, had intended Godolphin for a poet; for, with the exception of the love of glory, the poetical characteristics were rife within him; and over his whole past existence the dimness of unexpressed poetical sensation had clung and hovered. It was this which had deadened his soul to the active world, and wrapped him in the land of dreams; it was this which had induced that vague and restless dissatisfaction with the Actual which had brought the thirst for the Ideal; it was this which had made him fastidious in love, repining in pleasure, magnificent in luxury, seeking and despising all things in the same breath. There are many, perhaps, of this sort, who, having the poet's nature, have never found the poet's vent to his emotions; have wandered over the visionary world without chancing to discover the magic wand that was stored within the dark chamber of their mind, and would have reduced the visions into shape and substance. Alas! what existence can be more unfulfilled than that of one who has the soul of the poet and not the skill? who has the susceptibility and the craving, not the consolation or the reward?

But if this cloud of dreamlike emotion had so long hung over Godolphin, it began now to melt away from his heart; a clearer and distincter view of the large objects of life lay before him; and he felt that he was standing, half stunned and passive, in the great crisis of his fate.

The day was now fixed for their departure to Wendover, when Saville was taken alarmingly ill; Godolphin was sent for, late one evening. He found the soi-disant Epicurean at the point of death, but in perfect possession of his senses. The scene around him was emblematic of his life: save Godolphin, not a friend was by. Saville had some dozen or two of natural children—where were they? He had abandoned them to their fate: he knew not of their existence, nor they of his death. Lonely in his selfishness was he left to breathe out the small soul of a man of bon-ton! But I must do Saville the justice to say, that if he was without the mourners and the attendants that belonged to natural ties, he did not require them. His was no whimpering exit from life: the champagne was drained to the last drop; and Death, like the true boon companion, was about to shatter the empty glass.

"Well, my friend," said Saville, feebly, but pressing with weak fingers Godolphin's hand—"well, the game is up, the lights are going out, and presently the last guest will depart, and all be darkness!" here the doctor came to the bedside with a cordial. The dying man, before he took it, fixed upon the leech an eye which, although fast glazing, still retained something of its keen, searching shrewdness.

"Now tell me, my good sir, how many hours more can you keep in this—this breath?"

The doctor looked at Godolphin.

"I understand you," said Saville; you are shy on these points. Never be shy, my good fellow; it is inexcusable after twenty: besides, it is a bad compliment to my nerves—a gentleman is prepared for every event. Sir, it is only a roturier whom death, or anything else, takes by surprise. How many hours, then, can I live?"

"Not many, I fear, sir: perhaps until daybreak."

"My day breaks about twelve o'clock, p.m.," said Saville, as drily as his gasps would let him. "Very well;—give me the cordial;—don't let me go to sleep—I don't want to be cheated out of a minute. So, so—! I am better. You may withdraw, doctor. Let my spaniel come up. Bustle, Bustle!—poor fellow! poor fellow! Lie down, sir! be quiet! And now, Godolphin, a few words in farewell. I always liked you greatly; you know you were my protege, and you have turned out well. You have not been led away by the vulgar passions of politics, and place, and power. You have had power over power itself; you have not office, but you have fashion. You have made the greatest match in England; very prudently not marrying Constance Vernon, very prudently marrying Lady Erpingham. You are at the head and front of society; you have excellent taste, and spend your wealth properly. All this must make your conscience clear—a wonderful consolation! Always keep a sound conscience; it is a great blessing on one's death-bed—it is a great blessing tome in this hour, for I have played my part decently—eh?—I have enjoyed life, as much as so dull a possession can be enjoyed; I have loved, gamed, drunk, but I have never lost my character as a gentleman: thank Heaven, I have no remorse of that sort! Follow my example to the last and you will die as easily. I have left you my correspondence and my journal; you may publish them if you like; if not, burn them. They are full of amusing anecdotes; but I don't care for fame, as you well know—especially posthumous fame. Do as you please then, with my literary remains. Take care of my dog—'tis a good creature; and let me be quietly buried. No bad taste—no ostentation—no epitaph. I am very glad I die before the d—d Revolution that must come; I don't want to take wine with the Member for Holborn Bars. I am a type of a system; I expire before the system; my death is the herald of its fall."

With these expressions—not continuously uttered, but at short intervals—Saville turned away his face: his breathing became thick: he fell into the slumber he had deprecated; and, after about an hour's silence, died away as insensibly as an infant. Sic transit glories mundi!

The first living countenance beside the death-bed on which Godolphin's eye fell was that of Fanny Millinger; she (who had been much with Saville during his latter days, for her talk amused him, and her good-nature made her willing to amuse any one) had been, at his request, summoned also with Godolphin at the sudden turn of his disease. She was at the theatre at the time, and had only just arrived when the deceased had fallen into his last sleep. There, silent and shocked, she stood by the bed, opposite Godolphin. She had not stayed to change her stage-dress; and the tinsel and mock jewels glittered on the revolted eye of her quondam lover. What a type of the life just extinguished! What a satire on its mountebank artificialities!

Some little time after, she joined Godolphin in the desolate apartment below. She put her hand in his, and her tears—for she wept easily—flowed fast down her cheeks, washing away the lavish rouge which imperfectly masked the wrinkles that Time had lately begun to sow on a surface Godolphin had remembered so fair and smooth.

"Poor Saville!" said she, falteringly; "he died without a pang. Ah! he had the best temper possible."

Godolphin sat by the writing-table of the deceased, shading his brow with the hand which the actress left disengaged.

"Fanny," said he, bitterly, after a pause, "the world is indeed a stage. It has lost a consummate actor, though in a small part."

The saying was wrung from Godolphin—and was not said unkindly, though it seemed so—for he too had tears in his eyes.

"Ah," said she, the play-house has indeed taught us, in our youth, many things which the real world could not teach us better."

"Life differs from the play only in this," said Godolphin, some time afterwards; "it has no plot—all is vague, desultory, unconnected—till the curtain drops with the mystery unsolved."

Those were the last words that Godolphin ever addressed to the actress.

CHAPTER LXVI.

THE JOURNEY AND THE SURPRISE. — A WALK IN THE SUMMER NIGHT. — THE STARS AND THE ASSOCIATION THAT MEMORY MAKES WITH NATURE.

This event detained Godolphin some days longer in town. He saw the last rites performed to Saville, and he was present at the opening of the will.

As in life Saville had never lent a helping hand to the distressed, as he had mixed with the wealthy only, so now to the wealthy only was his wealth devoted. The rich Godolphin was his principal heir; not a word was even said about his illegitimate children, not an inquiry ordained towards his poor relations. In this, as in all the formula of his will, Saville followed the prescribed customs of the world.

Fast went the panting steeds that bore Constance and Godolphin from the desolate city. Bright was the summer sky, and green looked the smiling fields that lay on either side their road. Nature was awake and active. What a delicious contrast to the scenes of Art which they left behind! Constance exerted herself to the utmost to cheer the spirits of her companion, and succeeded. In the small compass which confined them together, their conversation flowed in confidence and intimate affection. Not since the first month of their union had they talked with less reserve and more entire love — only there was this difference in their topics they then talked of the future only, they now talked more of the past. They uttered many a fond regret over their several faults to each other; and, with clasped hands, congratulated themselves on their present reunion of heart. They allowed how much all things independent of affection had deceived them, and no longer exacting so much from love, they felt its real importance. Ah, why do all of us lose so many years in searching after happiness, but never inquiring into its nature! We are like one who collects the books of a thousand tongues, and knowing not their language, wonders why they do not delight him?

But still, athwart the mind of Constance one dark image would ever and anon obtrude itself; the solitary and mystic Lucilla, with her erring brain and forlorn fortunes, was not even in happiness to be forgotten. There were times, too, in that short journey, when she felt the tale of her interview with that unhappy being rise to her lips: but ever when she looked on the countenance of Godolphin, beaming with more heartfelt and homeborn gladness than she had seen for years, she could not bear the thought of seeing it darkened by the pain her story would inflict; and she shrank from embittering moments so precious to her heart.

All her endeavours to discover Lucilla had been in vain: but an unquiet presentiment that at any moment that discovery might be made, perhaps in the presence of Godolphin, constantly haunted her, and she even now looked painfully forth at each inn where they changed horses, lest the sad, stern features of the soothsayer should appear, and break that spell of happy quiet which now lay over the spirit of Godolphin.

It was towards the evening that their carriage slowly wound up a steep and long ascent. The sun yet wanted an hour to its setting; and at their right, its slant and mellowed beams fell over rich fields, green with the prodigal luxuriance of June, and intersected by hedges from which, proud and frequent, the oak and elm threw forth their lengthened shadows. On their left the grass less fertile, and the spaces less inclosed, were whitened with flocks of sheep; and far and soft came the bleating of the lambs upon their ear. They saw not the shepherd nor any living form; but from between the thicker groups of trees the chimneys of peaceful cottages peered forth, and gave to the pastoral serenity of the scene that still and tranquil aspect of life which alone suited it. The busy wheel in the heart of Constance was at rest, and Godolphin's soul, steeped in the luxury of the present hour, felt that delicious happiness which would be heaven could it outlive the hour.

"My Constance," whispered he, "why, since we return at last to these scenes, why should we ever leave them? Amidst them let us recall our youth!" Constance sighed, but with pleasure, and pressed Godolphin's hand to her lips.

And now they had gained the hill, a sudden colour flushed over Godolphin's cheek.

"Surely," said he, "I remember this view. Yonder valley! This is not the road to Wendover Castle; this—my father's home!—the same, and not the same!"

Yes! Below, basking in the western light, lay the cottage in which Godolphin's childhood had been passed. There was the stream rippling merrily; there the broken and fern-clad turf, with "its old hereditary trees;" but the ruins!—the shattered arch, the mouldering tower, were left indeed—but new arches, new turrets had arisen, and so dexterously blended with the whole that Godolphin might have fancied the hall of his forefathers restored—not indeed in the same vast proportions and cumbrous grandeur as of old, but still alike in shape and outline, and such even in size as would have contented the proud heart of its last owner. Godolphin's eyes turned inquiringly to Constance.

"It should have been more consistent with its ancient dimensions," said she; "but then it would have taken half our lives to have built it."

"But this must have been the work of years."

"It was."

"And your work, Constance?"

"For you."

"And it was for this that you hesitated when I asked you to consent to raising the money for the purchase of Lord — —'s collection?"

"Yes;—am I forgiven?"

"Dearest Constance," said Godolphin, flinging his arms around her, "how have I wronged you! During those very years, then, of our estrangement—during those very years in which I thought you indifferent, you were silently preparing this noble revenge on the injury I did you. Why, why did I not know this before? Why did you not save us both from so long a misunderstanding of each other?"

"Dearest Percy, I was to blame; but I always looked to this hour as to a pleasure of which I could not bear to rob myself. I always fancied that when this task was finished, and you could witness it, you would feel how uppermost you always were in my thoughts, and forgive me many faults from that consideration. I knew that I was executing your father's great wish; I knew that you always, although unconsciously, perhaps, sympathised in that wish. I only grieve that, as yet, it has been executed so imperfectly."

"But how," continued Godolphin, gazing on the new pile as they now neared the entrance, "how was it this never reached my ears through other quarters?"

"But it did, Percy; don't you remember our country neighbour, Dartmour, complimenting you on your intended improvements, and you fancied it was irony, and turned your back on the discomfited squire?"

They now drove under the gates surmounted with Godolphin's arms; and in a few minutes more, they were within the renovated halls of the Priory.

Perhaps it was impossible for Constance to have more sensibly touched and flattered Godolphin than by this surprise; it affected him far more than the political concession which to her had been so profound a sacrifice; for his early poverty had produced in him somewhat of that ancestral pride which the poor only can gracefully wear; and although the tie between his father and himself had not possessed much endearment, yet he had often, with the generosity that belonged to him, regretted that his parent had not survived to share in his present wealth, and to devote some portion of it to the realisation of those wishes which he had never been permitted to consummate. Godolphin, too, was precisely of a nature to appreciate the delicacy of Constance's conduct, and to be deeply penetrated by the thought that, while he was following a career so separate from hers, she, in the midst of all her ambitious projects, could pause to labour, unthanked and in concealment, for the delight of this hour's gratification to him: the delicacy and the forethought affected him the more, because they made not a part of the ordinary character of the high and absorbed ambition of Constance. He did not thank her much by words, but his looks betrayed all he felt, and Constance was overpaid.

Although the new portion of the building was necessarily not extensive, yet each chamber was of those grand proportions which suited the magnificent taste of Godolphin, and harmonised with the ancient ruins. Constance had shown her tact by leaving the ruins themselves (which it was profane to touch) unrestored; but so artfully were those connected with the modern addition, and thence with the apartments in the cottage, which she had not scrupled to remodel, that an effect was produced from the whole far more splendid than many Gothic buildings of greater extent and higher pretensions can afford. Godolphin wandered delightedly over the whole, charmed with the taste and judgment which presided over even the nicest arrangement.

"Why, where," said he, struck with the accurate antiquity of some of the details, "where learned you all these minutiae? You are as wise as Hope himself upon cornices and tables."

"I was forced to leave these things to others," answered Constance; "but I took care that they possessed the necessary science."

The night was exceedingly beautiful, and they walked forth under the summer moon among those grounds in which Constance had first seen Godolphin. They stood by the very rivulet—they paused at the very spot! On the murmuring bosom of the wave floated many a water-flower; and now and then a sudden splash, a sudden circle in the shallow stream, denoted the leap of the river-tyrant on his prey. There was a universal odor in the soft air; that delicate, that ineffable fragrance belonging to those midsummer nights which the rich English poetry might well people with Oberon and his fairies; the bat wheeled in many a ring along the air; but the gentle light bathed all things, and robbed his wanderings of the gloomier associations that belong to them; and ever, and ever, the busy moth darted to and fro among the flowers, or misled upwards by the stars whose beam allured it, wandered, like Desire after Happiness, in search of that light it might never reach. And those stars still, with their soft, unspeakable eyes of love, looked down upon Godolphin as of old, when, by the Italian lake, he roved with her for whom he had become the world itself. No, not now, nor ever, could he gaze upon those wan, mysterious orbs, and not feel the pang that reminded him of Lucilla! Between them and her was an affinity which his imagination could not sever. All whom we have loved have something in nature especially devoted to their memory; a peculiar flower, a breath of air, a leaf, a tone. What love is without some such association.

"Striking the electric chain wherewith we're bound"?

But the dim, and shadowy, and solemn stars were indeed meet remembrancers of Volktman's wild daughter; and so intimately was their light connected in Godolphin's breast with that one image, that their very softness had, to his eyes, something fearful and menacing—although as in sadness, not in anger.

CHAPTER LXVII

THE FULL RENEWAL OF LOVE.—HAPPINESS PRODUCES FEAR, "AND IN TO-DAY ALREADY WALKS TOMORROW."

Oh, First Love! well sang the gay minstrel of France, that we return again and again to thee. As the earth returns to its spring, and is green once more, we go back to the life of life and forget the seasons that have rolled between! Whether it was—perhaps so—that in the minds of both was a feeling that their present state was not fated to endure; whether they felt, in the deep calm they enjoyed, that the storm was already at hand; whether this was the truth I know not; but certain it is, that during the short time they remained at Godolphin Priory, previous to their earthly separation, Constance and Godolphin were rather like lovers for the first time united, than like those who have dragged on the chain for years. Their perfect solitude, the absence of all intrusion, so unlike the life they had long passed, renewed all that charm, that rapture in each other's society, which belong to the first youth of love. True, that this could not have endured long; but Fate suffered it to endure to the last of that tether which remained to their union. Constance was not again doomed to the severe and grating shock which the sense of estrangement brings to a woman's heart; she was sensible that Godolphin was never so entirely, so passionately her own, as towards the close of their mortal connection. Every thing around them breathed of their first love. This was that home of Godolphin's to which, from the splendid halls of Wendover, the young soul of the proud orphan had so often and so mournfully flown with a yearning and wistful interest: this was that spot in which he, awaking from the fever of the world, had fed his first dreams of her. The scene, the solitude, was as a bath to their love: it braced, it freshened, it revived its tone. They wandered, they read, they thought together; the air of the spot was an intoxication. The world around and without was agitated; they felt it not: the breakers of the great deep died in murmurs on their ear. Ambition lulled its voice to Constance; Godolphin had realised his visions of the ideal. Time had dimmed their young beauty, but their eyes saw it not; they were young, they were all beautiful, to each other.

And Constance hung on the steps of her lover—still let that name be his! She could not bear to lose him for a moment: a vague indistinctness of fear seized her if she saw him not. Again and again, in the slumbers of the night, she stretched forth her arms to feel that he was near; all her pride, her coldness seemed gone, as by a spell; she loved as the softest, the fondest, love. Are we, 0 Ruler of the future! imbued with the half-felt spirit of prophecy as the hour of evil approaches—the great, the fierce, the irremediable evil of a life? In this depth and intensity of their renewed passion, was there not something preternatural? Did they not tremble as they loved? They were on a spot to which the dark waters were slowly gathering; they clung to the Hour, for eternity was lowering round.

It was one evening that a foreboding emotion of this kind weighed heavily on Constance. She pressed Godolphin's hand in hers, and when he returned the pressure, she threw herself on his neck, and burst into tears. Godolphin was alarmed; he covered her cheek with kisses, he sought the cause of her emotion.

"There is no cause," answered Constance, recovering herself, but speaking in a faltering voice, "only I feel the impossibility that this happiness can last; its excess makes me shudder."

As she spoke, the wind rose and swept mournfully over the large leaves of the chestnut-tree beneath which they stood: the serene stillness of the evening seemed gone; an unquiet and melancholy spirit was loosened abroad, and the chill of the sudden change which is so frequent to our climate, came piercingly upon them.

Godolphin was silent for some moments, for the thought found a sympathy in his own.

"And is it truly so?" he said at last; "is there really to be no permanent happiness for us below? Is pain always to tread the heels of pleasure? Are we never to say the harbour is reached, and we are safe? No, my Constance," he added, warming into the sanguine vein that traversed even his most desponding moods, "no! let us not cherish this dark belief; there is no experience for the future; one hour lies to the next; if what has been seem thus chequered, it is no type of what may be. We have discovered in each other that world that was long lost to our eyes; we cannot lose it again; death only can separate us!"

"Ah, death!" said Constance, shuddering.

"Do not recoil at that word, my Constance, for we are yet in the noon of life; why bring, like the Egyptian, the spectre to the feast? And, after all, if death come while we thus love, it is better than change and time—better than custom which palls—better than age which chills. Oh!" continued Godolphin, passionately, "oh! if this narrow shoal and sand of time be but a breathing-spot in the great heritage of immortality, why cheat ourselves with words so vague as life and death? What is the difference? At most, the entrance in and the departure from one scene in our wide career. How many scenes are left to us! We do but hasten our journey, not close it. Let us believe this, Constance, and cast from us all fear of our disunion."

As he spoke, Constance's eyes were fixed upon his face, and the deep calm that reigned there sank into her soul, and silenced its murmurs. The thought of futurity is that which Godolphin (because it is so with all idealists) must have revolved with the most frequent fervour; but it was a thought which he so rarely touched upon, that it was the first and only time Constance ever heard it breathed from his lips.

They turned into the house; and the mark is still in that page of the volume which they read, where the melodious accents of Godolphin died upon the heart of Constance. Can she ever turn to it again?

CHAPTER LXVIII.

THE LAST CONVERSATION BETWEEN GODOLPHIN AND CONSTANCE. — HIS THOUGHTS AND SOLITARY WALK AMIDST THE SCENES OF HIS YOUTH. — THE LETTER. — THE DEPARTURE.

They had denied themselves to all the visitors who had attacked the Priory; but on their first arrival, they had deemed it necessary to conciliate their neighbours by concentrating into one formal act of hospitality all those social courtesies which they could not persuade themselves to relinquish their solitude in order singly to perform. Accordingly, a day had been fixed for one grand fete at the Priory; it was to follow close on the election, and be considered as in honour of that event. The evening for this gala succeeded that which I have recorded in the last chapter. It was with great reluctance that they prepared themselves to greet this sole interruption of their seclusion; and they laughed, although they did not laugh cordially, at the serious annoyance which the giving a ball was for the first time to occasion to persons who had been giving balls for a succession of years.

The day was remarkably still and close; the sun had not once pierced through the dull atmosphere, which was charged with the yet silent but gathering thunder; and as the evening came on, the sullen tokens of an approaching storm became more and more loweringly pronounced.

"We shall not, I fear, have propitious weather for our festival to-night," said Godolphin; "but after a general election, people's nerves are tolerably hardened: what are the petty fret and tumult of nature, lasting but an hour, to the angry and everlasting passions of men?"

"A profound deduction from a wet night, dear Percy," said Constance, smiling.

"Like our friend C— —," rejoined Godolphin, in the same vein; "I can philosophise on the putting on one's gloves, you know:" and therewith their conversation flowed into a vein singularly contrasted with the character of the coming events. Time fled on as they were thus engaged until Constance started up, surprised at the lateness of the hour, to attend the duties of the toilette.

"Wear this, dearest," said Godolphin, taking a rose from a flower-stand by the window, "in memory of that ball at Wendover Castle, which although itself passed bitterly enough for me, has yet left so many happy recollections." Constance put the rose into her bosom; its leaves were then all fresh and brilliant—so were her prospects for the future. He kissed her forehead as they parted;—they parted for the last time.

Godolphin, left alone, turned to the window, which, opening to the ground, invited him forth among the flowers that studded the grass-plots which sloped away to the dark and unwavering trees that girded the lawn. That pause of nature which precedes a storm ever had a peculiar attraction to his mind; and instinctively he sauntered from the house, wrapped in the dreaming, half-developed thought which belonged to his temperament. Mechanically he strayed on until he found himself beside the still lake which the hollows of the dismantled park embedded. There he paused, gazing unconsciously on the gloomy shadows which fell from the arches of the Priory and the tall trees around. Not a ripple stirred the broad expanse of waters; the birds had gone to rest; no sound, save the voice of the distant brook that fed the lake beside which, on the first night of his return to his ancestral home, he had wandered with Constance, broke the universal silence. That voice was never mute. All else might be dumb; but that living stream, rushing through its rocky bed, stilled not its repining music. Like the soul of the landscape is the gush of a fresh stream; it knows no sleep, no pause; it works for ever—the life, the cause of life to all around. The great frame of nature may repose, but the spirit of the waters rests not for a moment. As the soul of the landscape is the soul of man, in our deepest slumbers its course glides on, and works unsilent, unslumbering, through its destined channel.

With slow step and folded arms Godolphin moved along. The well-remembered scenes of his childhood were all before him; the wild verdure of the fern, the broken ground, with its thousand mimic mounts and valleys, the deep dell overgrown with matted shrubs and dark as a wizard's cave; the remains of many a stately vista, where the tender green of the lime showed forth, even in that dusky light, beneath the richer leaves of the chestnut; all was familiar and home-breathing to his mind. Fragments of boyish verse, forgotten for years, rose hauntingly to his remembrance, telling of wild thoughts, unsatisfied dreams, disappointed hopes.

"But I am happy at last," said he aloud; "yes, happy. I have passed that bridge of life which divides us from the follies of youth; and better prospects, and nobler desires, extend before me. What a world of wisdom in that one saying of Radclyffe's, 'Benevolence is the sole cure to idealism;' to live for others draws us from demanding miracles for ourselves. What duty as yet have I fulfilled? I renounced ambition as unwise, and with it I renounced wisdom itself. I lived for pleasure—I lived the life of disappointment. Without one vicious disposition, I have fallen into a hundred vices; I have never been actively selfish, yet always selfish. I nursed high thoughts—for what end? A poet in heart, a voluptuary in life. If mine own interest came into clear collision with that of another, mine I would have sacrificed, but I never asked if the whole course of my existence was not that of a war with the universal interest. Too thoughtful to be without a leading principle in life, the one principle I adopted has been one error. I have tasted all that imagination can give to earthly possession: youth, health, liberty, knowledge, love, luxury, pomp. Woman was my first passion,—what woman have I wooed in vain? I imagined that my career hung upon Constance's breath— Constance loved and refused me. I attributed my errors to that refusal; Constance became mine—how have I retrieved them? A vague, a dim, an unconfessed remorse has pursued me in the memory of Lucilla; yet, why not have redeemed that fault to her by good to others? What is penitence not put into action, but the great fallacy in morals? A sin to one, if irremediable, can only be compensated by a virtue to some one else. Yet was I to blame in my conduct to Lucilla? Why should conscience so haunt me at that name? Did I not fly her? Was it not herself who compelled our union? Did I not cherish, respect, honour, forbear with her, more than I have since with my wedded Constance? Did I not resolve to renounce Constance herself, when most loved, for Lucilla's sake alone? Who prevented that sacrifice—who deserted me—who carved out her own separate life?—Lucilla herself. No, so far, my sin is light. But ought I not to have left all things to follow her, to discover her, to force upon her an independence from want, or possibly from crime? Ah, there was my sin, and the sin of my nature; the sin, too, of the children of the world—passive sin. I could sacrifice my happiness, but not my indolence; I was not ungenerous, I was inert. But is it too late? Can I not yet search, discover her, and remove from my mind the anxious burthen which her remembrance imposes on it? For, oh, one thought of remorse linked with the being who has loved us, is more intolerable to the conscience than the gravest crime!"

Muttering such thoughts, Godolphin strayed on until the deepening night suddenly recalled his attention to the lateness of the hour. He turned to the house and entered his own apartment. Several of the guests had already come. Godolphin was yet dressing, when a servant knocked at the door and presented him with a note.

"Lay it on the table," said he to the valet; "it is probably some excuse about the ball."

"Sir," said the servant, "a lad has just brought it from S— —," naming a village about four miles distant; "and says he is to wait for an answer. He was ordered to ride as fast as possible."

With some impatience Godolphin took up the note; but the moment his eye rested on the writing, it fell from his hands; his cheek, his lips, grew as white as death; his heart seemed to refuse its functions; it was literally as if life stood still for a moment, as by the force of a sudden poison. With a strong effort he recovered himself, tore open the note, and read as follows:

"Percy Godolphin, the hour has arrived-once more we shall meet. I summon you, fair love, to that meeting—the bed of death. Come! Lucilla Volktman."

"Don't alarm the countess," said Godolphin to his servant, in a very low, calm voice; "bring my horse to the postern, and send the bearer of this note to me."

The messenger appeared—a rough country lad, of about eighteen or twenty.

"You brought this note?"

"I did, your honour."

"From whom?"

"Why, a sort of a strange lady as is lying at the 'Chequers,' and not expected to live. She be mortal bad, sir, and do run on awesome."

Godolphin pressed his hands convulsively together.

"And how long has she been there?"

"She only came about two hours since, sir; she came in a chaise, sir, and was taken so ill, that we sent for the doctor directly. He says she can't get over the night."

Godolphin walked to and fro, without trusting himself to speak, for some minutes. The boy stood by the door, pulling about his hat, and wondering, and staring, and thoroughly stupid.

"Did she come alone?"

"Eh, your honour?"

"Was no one with her?"

"Oh, yes! a little nigger girl: she it was sent me with the letter."

"The horse is ready, sir," said the servant; "but had you not better have the carriage brought out? It looks very black; it must rain shortly, sir; and the ford between this and S— — is dangerous to cross in so dark a night."

"Peace!" cried Godolphin, with flashing eyes, and a low convulsive laugh.
"Shall I ride to that death-bed at my ease and leisure?"

He strode rapidly down the stairs, and reached the small postern door: it was a part of the old building: one of the grooms held his impatient horse — the swiftest in his splendid stud; and the dim but flaring light, held by another of the servitors, streamed against the dull heavens and the imperfectly seen and frowning ruins of the ancient pile.

Godolphin, unconscious of all around, and muttering to himself, leaped on his steed: the fire glinted from the coursers hoofs; and thus the last lord of that knightly race bade farewell to his father's halls. Those words which he had muttered, and which his favourite servant caught and superstitiously remembered, were the words in Lucilla's note — "The hour has arrived!"

CHAPTER THE LAST.

A DREAD MEETING. — THE STORM. — THE CATASTROPHE.

On the humble pallet of the village inn lay the broken form of the astrologer's expiring daughter. The surgeon of the place sat by the bedside, dismayed and terrified, despite his hardened vocation, by the wild words and ghastly shrieks that ever and anon burst from the lips of the dying woman. The words were, indeed, uttered in a foreign tongue unfamiliar to the leech, a language not ordinarily suited to inspire terror; the language of love, and poetry, and music, the language of the sweet South. But, uttered in that voice where the passions of the soul still wrestled against the gathering weakness of the frame, the soft syllables sounded harsh and fearful; and the dishevelled locks of the sufferer — the wandering fire of the sunken eyes — the distorted gestures of the thin, transparent arms, gave fierce effect to the unknown words, and betrayed the dark strength of the delirium which raged upon her.

One wretched light on the rude table opposite the bed broke the gloom of the mean chamber; and across the window flashed the first lightnings of the storm about to break. By the other side of the bed sat, mute, watchful, tearless, the Moorish girl, who was Lucilla's sole attendant — her eyes fixed on the sufferer with faithful, unwearying love; her ears listening, with all the quick sense of her race, to catch, amidst the growing noises of the storm, and the tread of hurrying steps below, the expected sound of the hoofs that should herald Godolphin's approach.

Suddenly, as if exhausted by the paroxysm of her disease, Lucilla's voice sank into silence; and she lay so still, so motionless, that, but for the faint and wavering pulse of the hand, which the surgeon was now suffered to hold, they might have believed the tortured spirit was already released. This torpor lasted for some minutes, when, raising herself up, as a bright gleam of intelligence stole over the hollow cheeks, Lucilla put her finger to her lips, smiled, and said, in a low, clear voice, "Hark! he comes!"

The Moor crept across the chamber, and opening the door, stood there in a listening attitude. She, as yet, heard not the tread of the speeding charger; — a moment, and it smote her ear; a moment more it halted by the inn door: the snort of the panting horse—the rush of steps—Percy Godolphin was in the room—was by the bedside—the poor sufferer was in his arms; and softened, thrilled, overpowered, Lucilla resigned herself to that dear caress; she drank in the sobs of his choked voice; she felt still, as in happier days, burning into her heart, the magic of his kisses. One instant of youth, of love, of hope, broke into that desolate and fearful hour, and silent and scarcely conscious tears gushed from her aching eyes, and laved, as it were, the burthen and the agony from her heart.

The Moor traversed the room, and, laying one hand on the surgeon's shoulder, pointed to the door. Lucilla and Godolphin were alone.

"Oh!" said he, at last finding voice, "is it thus—thus we meet? But say not that you are dying, Lucilla! have mercy, mercy upon your betrayer, your——"

Here he could utter no more; he sank beside her, covering his face with his hands, and sobbing bitterly.

The momentary lucid interval for Lucilla had passed away; the maniac rapture returned, although in a wild and solemn shape.

"Blame not yourself," said she, earnestly; "the remorseless stars are the sole betrayers: yet, bright and lovely as they once seemed when they assured me of a bond between thee and me, I could not dream that their still and shining lore could forebode such gloomy truths. Oh, Percy! since we parted, the earth has not been as the earth to me: the Natural has left my life; a weird and roving spirit has entered my breast, and filled my brain, and possessed my thoughts, and moved every spring of my existence: the sun and the air, the green herb, the freshness and glory of the world, have been covered with a mist in which only dim shapes of dread were shadowed forth. But thou, my love, on whose breast I have dreamed such blessed dreams, wert not to blame. No! the power that crushes we cannot accuse: the heavens are above the reach of our reproach; they smile upon our agony; they bid the seasons roll on, unmoved and unsympathising, above our broken hearts. And what has been my course since your last kiss on these dying lips? Godolphin,"— and here Lucilla drew herself apart from him, and writhed, as with some bitter memory,—"these lips have felt other kisses, and these ears have drunk unhallowed sounds, and wild revelry and wilder passion have made me laugh over the sepulchre of my soul. But I am a poor creature; pour, poor—mad, Percy—mad—they tell me so!" Then, in the sudden changes incident to her disease, Lucilla continued—"I saw your bride, Percy, when your bore her from Rome, and the wheels of your bridal carriage swept over me, for I flung myself in their way; but they scratched me not; the bright demons above ordained otherwise, and I wandered over the world; but you shall know not," added Lucilla, with a laugh of dreadful levity, "whither or with whom, for we must have concealments, my love, as you will confess; and I strove to forget you, and my brain sank in the effort. I felt my frame withering, and they told me my doom was fixed, and I resolved to come to England, and look on my first love once more; so I came, and I saw you, Godolphin; and I knew, by the wrinkles in your brow, and the musing thought in your eye, that your proud lot had not brought you content. And then there came to me a stately shape, and I knew it for her for whom you had deserted me: she told me, as you tell me, to live, to forget the past. Mockery, mockery! But my heart is proud as hers, Percy, and I would not stoop to the kindness of a triumphant rival; and I fled, what matters it whither? But listen, Percy, listen; my woes have made me wise in that science which is not of heart, and I knew that you and I must meet once more, and that that meeting would be in this hour; and I counted, minute by minute, with a savage gladness, the days that were to bring on this interview and my death!" Then raising her voice into a wild shriek—"Beware, beware, Percy!-the rush of waters is on my ear-the splash, the gurgle!—Beware!— your last hour, also; is at hand!"

From the moment in which she uttered these words, Lucilla relapsed into her former frantic paroxysms. Shriek followed shriek; she appeared to know none around her, not even Godolphin. With throes and agony the soul seemed to wrench itself from the frame. The hours swept on—midnight came—clear and distinct the voice of the clock below reached that chamber.

"Hush!" cried Lucilla, starting. "Hush!" and just at that moment, through the window opposite, the huge clouds, breaking in one spot, discovered high and far above them a solitary star.

"Thine, thine, Godolphin!" she shrieked forth, pointing to the lonely orb; "it summons thee;—farewell, but not for long!"

* * * * * * * * * * * * * *

The Moor rushed forward with a loud cry; she placed her hand on Lucilla's bosom; the heart was still, the breath was gone, the fire had vanished from the ashes: that strange unearthly spirit was perhaps with the stars for whose mysteries it had so vainly yearned.

Down fell the black rain in torrents; and far from the mountains you might hear the rushing of the swollen streams, as they poured into the bosom of the valleys. The sullen, continued mass of cloud was broken, and the vapours hurried fast and louring over the heavens, leaving now and then a star to glitter forth ere again "the jaws of darkness did devour it up." At the lower verge of the horizon, the lightning flashed fierce, but at lingering intervals; the trees rocked and groaned beneath the rain and storm; and, immediately above the bowed head of a solitary horseman, broke the thunder that, amidst the whirl of his own emotions, he scarcely heard.

Beside a stream, which the rains had already swelled, was a gipsy encampment; and as some of the dusky itinerants, waiting perhaps the return of a part of their band from a predatory excursion, cowered over the flickering fires in their tent, they perceived the horseman rapidly approaching the stream.

"See to yon gentry cove," cried one of the band; "'tis the same we saw in the forenight crossing the ford above. He has taken a short cut, the buzzard! and will have to go round again to the ford; a precious time to be gallivanting about!"

"Pish!" said an old hag; "I love to see the proud ones tasting the bitter wind and rain as we bear alway; 'tis but a mile longer round to the ford. I wish it was twenty."

"Hallo!" cried the first speaker; "the fool takes to the water. He'll be drowned; the banks are too high and rough to land man or horse yonder. Hallo!" and with that painful sympathy which the hardest feel at the imminent peril of another when immediately subjected to their eyes, the gipsy ran forth into the pelting storm, shouting to the traveller to halt. For one moment Godolphin's steed still shrunk back from the rushing tide: deep darkness was over the water; and the horseman saw not the height of the opposite banks. The shout of the gipsy sounded to his ear like the cry of the dead whom he had left: he dashed his heels into the sides of the reluctant horse, and was in the stream.

"Light—light the torches!" cried the gipsy; and in a few moments the banks were illumined with many a brand from the fire, which the rain however almost instantly extinguished; yet, by that momentary light, they saw the noble animal breasting the waters, and perceived that Godolphin, discovering by the depth his mistake, had already turned the horse's head in the direction of the ford: they could see no more, but they shouted to Godolphin to turn back to the place from which he had plunged; and, in a few minutes afterwards, they heard, several yards above, the horse clambering up the rugged banks, which there were steep and high, and crushing the boughs that clothed the ascent. They thought, at the same time, that they distinguished also the splash of a heavy substance in the waves; but they fancied it some detached fragment of earth or stone, and turned to their tent, in the belief that the daring rider had escaped the peril he had so madly incurred. That night the riderless steed of Godolphin arrived at the porch of the Priory, where Constance, alarmed, pale, breathless, stood exposed to the storm, awaiting the return of Godolphin, or the messengers she had despatched in search of him.

At daybreak his corpse was found by the shallows of the ford; and the mark of violence across the temples, as of some blow, led them to guess that in scaling the banks his head had struck against one of the tossing boughs that overhung them, and the blow had precipitated him into the waters.

LETTER FROM CONSTANCE, COUNTESS OF ERPINGHAM, TO * * * .

August, 1832.

"I have read the work you have so kindly compiled from the papers transmitted to your care, and from your own intimate knowledge of those to whom they relate;—you have in much fulfilled my wishes with singular success. On the one hand, I have been anxious that a History should be given to the world, from which lessons so deep and, I firmly believe, salutary, may be generally derived: on the other hand, I have been anxious that it should be clothed in such disguises, that the names of the real actors in the drama should be for ever a secret. Both these objects you have attained. It is impossible I think, for any one to read the book about to be published, without being impressed with the truth of the moral it is intended to convey, and without seeing, by a thousand infallible signs, that its spring and its general course have flowed from reality and not fiction. Yet have you, by a few light alterations and addition, managed to effect that concealment of names and persons, which is due no less to the living than to the memory of the dead.

"So far I thank you from my heart: but in one point yon have utterly failed. You have done no justice to the noble character you meant to delineate under the name of Godolphin; you have drawn his likeness with a harsh and cruel pencil; you have enlarged on the few weaknesses he might have possessed, until you have made them the foreground of the portrait; and his vivid generosity, his high honour, his brilliant intellect, the extraordinary stores of his mind, you have left in shadow. Oh, God! that for such a being such a destiny was reserved! and in the prime of life, just when his mind had awakened to a sense of its own powers and their legitimate objects! What a fatal system of things, that could for thirty-seven years have led away, by the pursuits and dissipations of a life suited but to the beings be despised, a genius of such an order, a heart of such tender emotions![1] But on this subject I cannot, cannot write. I must lay down the pen: to-morrow I will try and force myself to resume it.

"Well, then, I say, you have not done justice to him. I beseech you to remodel that character, and atone to the memory of one, whom none ever saw but to admire, or knew but to love.

"Of me,—of me, the vain, the scheming, the proud, the unfeminine cherishes of bitter thoughts, of stern designs,—of me, on the other hand, how flattering is the picture you have drawn! In that flattery is my sure disguise; therefore, I will not ask you to shade it into the poor and unlovely truth. But while, with agony and shame, I feel that you have rightly described that seeming neglectfulness of one no more, which sprang from the pride that believed itself neglected, you have not said enough—no, not one millionth part enough—of the real love that I constantly bore to him: the only soft and redeeming portion of my nature. But who can know, who can describe what another feels? Even I knew not what I felt, until death taught it me.

"Since I have read the whole book, one thought constantly haunts me—the strangeness that I should survive his loss; that the stubborn strings of my heart have not been broken long since; that I live, and live, too, amidst the world! Ay, but not one of the world; with that consciousness I sustain myself in the petty and sterile career of life. Shut out henceforth and for ever, from all the tenderer feelings that belong to my sex; without mother, husband, child, or friend; un-loved and unloving, I support myself by the belief that I have done the little suffered to my sex in expediting the great change which is advancing on the world; and I cheer myself by the firm assurance that, sooner or later, a time must come, when those vast disparities in life which have been fatal, not to myself alone, but to all I have admired and loved; which render the great heartless, and the lowly servile; which make genius either an enemy to mankind or the vic-tim to itself; which debase the energetic purpose; which fritter away the ennobling sentiment; which cool the heart and fetter the capaci-ties, and are favorable only to the general development of the Me-diocre and the Lukewarm, shall, if never utterly removed, at least be smoothed away into more genial and unobstructed elements of society. Alas! it is with an aching eye that we look abroad for the only solace, the only occupation of life,—Solitude at home, and Memory at our hearth."

THE END.

[1] The reader will acquit me of the charge of injustice to Godol-phin's character when he arrives at this sentence; it conveys exactly the impression that my delineation, faithful to truth, is intended to convey—the influences of our actual world on the ideal and imagi-native order of mind, when that mind is without the stimulus of pursuits at once practical and ennobling.